Eric Maddern's storytelling has taken him all over Britain to schools, colleges, galleries, forests, gardens, museums and festivals. He lives in western Snowdonia where he has created Cae Mabon, an eco-retreat centre which was, in 2008, declared the number one natural building project in the UK. Eric's other titles for Frances Lincoln are
Death in a Nut, Nail Soup, Cow on the Roof, Earth Story,
The King with Horse's Ears, Spirit of the Forest, Rainbow Bird, Life Story,
Curious Clownfish and *The King and the Seed.*

Frané Lessac is an internationally known American artist who has exhibited her paintings in London, Paris, New York and Los Angeles. From film school in California she went on to study Caribbean culture on the island of Monserrat. She has worked on many children's projects to date. The other books she has illustrated for Frances Lincoln are *The Turtle and the Island* and *Maui and the Big Fish* (both by Barbara Ker Wilson), and she also contributed to *We are all Born Free*. She lives in Western Australia.

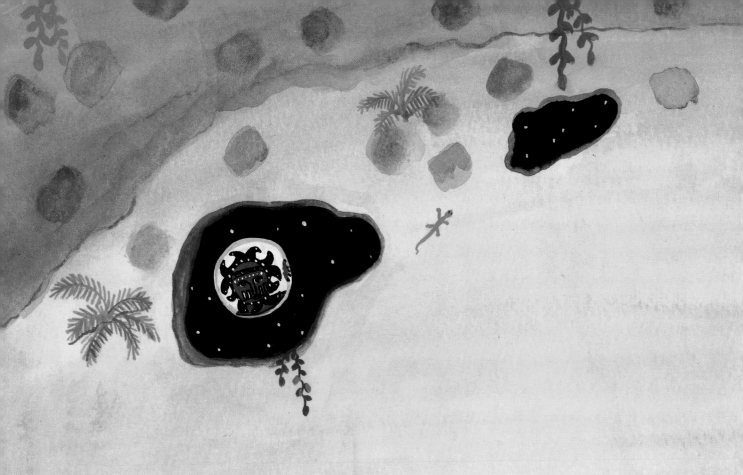

For respect and goodwill
between the peoples of the Earth – E.M.
For Mark – F.L.

The Fire Children copyright © Frances Lincoln Limited 1993
Text copyright © Eric Maddern 1993
This story is based on a West African creation myth
adapted from *Gods and Men: Myths and Legends from the World's Religions*,
retold by John R. Bailey, Kenneth McLeish and David Spearman
(Oxford University Press) 1981
Illustrations copyright © Frané Lessac 1993

First published in Great Britain in 1993 by
Frances Lincoln Children's Books, 4 Torriano Mews,
Torriano Avenue, London NW5 2RZ
www.franceslincoln.com

This edition first published in Great Britain and in the USA in 2006

A catalogue record for this book is available from the British Library.

ISBN 978-1-84507-514-9

Set in Bembo Roman

Printed in Shenzhen, Guangdong, China by WKT Co. Ltd. in November 2009

10 12 14 16 18 19 17 15 13 11

THE FIRE CHILDREN

A West African folk tale

Retold by Eric Maddern
Illustrated by Frané Lessac

FRANCES LINCOLN
CHILDREN'S BOOKS

Long ago Nyame, the great sky-god, lived alone in the wide blue sky. One day he took a basket and filled it with earth, trees, flowers, insects and birds, and he hung it in the sky. That basket was the Earth.

Then he made a round trapdoor in the sky so that he could climb down to visit the earth, with little holes so that the light could shine through when the trapdoor was shut. The trapdoor and holes were the moon and the stars.

One day Nyame was looking through his trapdoor moon admiring the Earth down below. But deep inside him two little spirit people were curious. They wanted to see what was going on.

So they climbed up Nyame's throat, into his mouth, over his tongue and were just looking through his teeth when he let out a tremendous sneeze.

The two spirit people, Kwaku Ananse and Aso Yaa,
went flying out through the trapdoor,
down,
  down,
    down,

and landed with a bump on the Earth.

They picked themselves up and looked around at the tall trees and hanging vines, the dark pools and splashing streams, the brilliant birds flashing through the leaves. Nearby they found a warm cave and decided to make it their home.

Each day they went outside to explore, to sing with the wind and dance with the falling leaves.

One day Aso Yaa was lonely, and she stayed at home in the
cave. When Kwaku Ananse returned she had a big smile on
her face.

"Oh Aso Yaa of many moods," he said, "when I left this
morning you were sad. Now you are glowing like a hibiscus
flower. What is it?"

"I have an idea," she said.

"Not another idea!" said Kwaku Ananse. "Last time you
had an idea we were inside Nyame. Now look where we are!"

"Listen," said Aso Yaa. "It will not hurt you to listen."

"First we take some clay," Aso Yaa began, "and mould it into little shapes just like us, with arms and legs and heads. Then we bake them in the fire and when they are cooked we breathe life into them. We could call them children."

"That's not a bad idea," said Kwaku Ananse. So the next day Aso Yaa dug up clay outside the cave and they made a hot glowing fire. Then they shaped little figures like themselves and put them on the fire to bake.

Suddenly, they heard crashing footsteps outside in the forest. Nyame had come to visit. Frightened that they were doing wrong, Kwaku Ananse and Aso Yaa snatched the little clay figures from the fire, wrapped them in leaves and hid them at the back of the cave.

Nyame's face appeared at the mouth of the cave.

"Well, my spirit people," he said, "are you enjoying my Earth?"

"Oh yes, Nyame," they replied.

"Are you being good?"

"Oh yes, Nyame," they answered, "we're being very good."

"Well, take good care of everything I have made," Nyame boomed, and then he disappeared.

Next day, Aso Yaa made a new batch of clay children, but no sooner had they begun to bake than Nyame was back again.

This time the spirit people had no time to take out the little figures. Instead, they stood in front of the fire hiding their work. And this time Nyame stayed talking for a long time. Maybe he suspected something. By the time he was gone, the clay children were baked quite black.

And so it went on. Every day they made more shapes and put them in the fire. And every day Nyame called to see them. Sometimes they heard him coming and were able to take the children out of the fire. Sometimes they had to leave them in the fire until he had gone.

But at last Nyame climbed back through the trapdoor moon and into the sky world above.

Then Kwaku Ananse and Aso Yaa spread out all the fire children. Some were hardly cooked at all and were white. Some were rosy pink, some honey yellow, some dusky red, some nut brown – and some midnight black. Kwaku Ananse and Aso Yaa loved them all, because they were their children.

Now the spirit people breathed life into the fire children. One by one they awoke, yawned, stretched and opened their eyes, just like children waking up in the morning. Then they stood up and went off to play.

Years later, when the fire children grew up, they wandered to all corners of the Earth and had children of their own. And their children had children.

And that is why today the Earth is filled with people of many different colours – black, white, red, brown, yellow and pink. Kwaku Ananse and Aso Yaa love them still.

They always will.

MORE TITLES FROM
FRANCES LINCOLN CHILDREN'S BOOKS

The King with Horse's Ears
Eric Maddern
Illustrated by Paul Hess

No-one knows about King Mark's ears except his barber.
Keeping the secret eventually drives him to the doctor,
who advises him to whisper it to the ground.
But sooner or later, truth will out…

Spirit of the Forest
Tree Tales from around the World
Helen East and Eric Maddern
Illustrated by Alan Marks

Trees are symbols of life itself. We cut them down at our peril.
Here is a leafy anthology of 12 traditional tales from all over the
Earth's surface from Native North America to New Guinea
and from Wales to Nepal.

Maui and the Big Fish
Barbara Ker Wilson
Illustrated by Frané Lessac

Long ago when the world was new and little Maui was born,
the great god Tama carried him away to the underworld to learn magic.
When Maui came back, his brothers made fun of him and
wouldn't take him deep-sea fishing. They stole away on a fishing trip,
thinking he was still asleep…

Frances Lincoln titles are available from all good bookshops.
You can also buy books and find out more about your favourite titles,
authors and illustrators on our website: www.franceslincoln.com